BEATRICE BLY'S RULES FOR SPIES

THE MISSING HAMSTER

Sue Fliess · Illustrated by Beth Mills

PIXEL ✚ INK

To Kerry and Bec, for solving life's mysteries with me —S.F.

To Jason, a super ~~spy~~ guy! —B.M.

PIXEL+INK

Text copyright © 2021 by Sue Fliess
Illustrations copyright © 2021 by Beth Mills
All rights reserved
Pixel+Ink is a division of TGM Development Corp.
Printed and bound in December 2020 at Leo Paper, Heshan, China
Cover and interior design by Georgia Morrissey
www.pixelandinkbooks.com
Library of Congress Control Number: 2020940460
ISBN 978-1-64595-028-8
eBook ISBN 978-1-64595-030-1
First Edition
1 3 5 7 9 10 8 6 4 2

Beatrice Bly was no ordinary spy.

Beatrice was a . . . SUPER SPY!

She had the skills.

She knew the rules . . .

SUPER SPY RULES

* Never reveal your spy identity (OK to tell your best friend)

* Observe and write down everything

* Be quiet (<u>no flip-flops!!!</u>)

. . . and she had plenty of missions.

Like the time she took on OPERATION WIZARD CLOAK.

Beatrice explored.

She observed.

She took notes.

She followed her spy hunch and

"Ta-da!"

Beatrice also solved
MISSION MYSTERY SQUEAK.

AH-HA!!

And she tackled

PROJECT REMOTE CONTROL

with ease.

But Beatrice felt ready
for even bigger missions.

The next day, Beatrice sprang off the bus, dashed into school, and walked at super spy speed to her classroom. "Record time!" she said, checking her watch.

"Good morning, class," said Miss Leland.
"Before we start, I have some troubling news.
Edgar, our classroom hamster, is missing."

The class gasped.

The hairs on Beatrice's arms stood up.

A mission.

"He can't have gone far," said Miss Leland.
"Let's take a few minutes to look for him."

"Poor Edgar!" said Beatrice's best friend Nora.

"What if he's lost?"

"Or stolen!" said Beatrice.

"Or someone let him out!"

"A third-grader did free all the ants from the ant farm in science last week," said Beatrice. "Wherever Edgar is, he must be hungry."

"We all loved feeding him fruits and veggies," said Nora. "What will he eat now?"

"Don't worry," said Beatrice. "I've been
training for this my whole life."
She pulled out her notebook:

Beatrice looked for clues.

She kept an eye on her classmates. And even though she didn't think anyone would steal Edgar, any decent spy knew that in the beginning, *everyone* is a suspect.

She investigated the scene.

She wrote in her notebook:

Unlatched Door
Mystery Leaves

By the end of class, there was still no sign of Edgar. "Keep a lookout for him today," said Miss Leland. "I'll tell the other teachers."

In PE, Nora said, "I heard there's a fancy luncheon today
in the teachers lounge."

"How can they celebrate at a time like this?" said Beatrice.

"Yeah, and they'll probably have donuts," said Nora.

By recess, Edgar was still missing. Beatrice went over her notes.

"Any luck with MISSION MISSING HAMSTER?" whispered Nora.

"*Super spy* mission," Beatrice whispered back. "And no. Nothing."

"Bummer," said Nora. "I even saved my carrots for him, just in case."

"If you were a hungry hamster," asked Beatrice, "where would you go?"

They looked at each other. "The cafeteria!"

Thankful she had her best spy shoes on, Beatrice pulled her hair
back, crept into the school, and slipped on her sunglasses.
Then, using her stealthiest spy moves, she slinked down the hall.

But before she got to the cafeteria, she noticed something familiar.

"Mystery leaves," said Beatrice. Then she saw she was standing in front of the teachers lounge.

"The luncheon!" said Beatrice. But no students were allowed inside. Secret teacher-y things happened there.

Yet Beatrice knew she had to follow her spy instincts. And any decent spy tracks down all leads.

She looked both ways and peeked in.
No teachers . . . for now.
She slid inside.

Sure enough, the teachers were about to have a feast.

Beatrice observed:
a sandwich platter,
balloons,
donuts,

and . . .

EDGAR!

Beatrice carefully placed him in her backpack.

But as she opened the door to leave . . .

"Beatrice!"

"Miss Leland!"

"Why are you here? Is everything okay?"

"More than okay," said Beatrice. "Look who I found."

"Oh, Edgar, thank goodness you're safe!" said Miss Leland. "Beatrice, how did you know he'd be here?"

"He followed the food . . . and I followed a hunch."

"Well, I don't blame him," said Miss Leland. "I took a few strawberries from here today, too, and even snuck a couple to Edgar this morning. Don't tell anyone, okay?"

"If you don't tell anyone I
snuck into the teachers lounge,"
said Beatrice.
"Deal."

Back in the classroom, Beatrice set Edgar
in his cage, then closed and latched his door.
The class cheered.

"This calls for a celebration!" said Miss Leland.

"Edgar *and* donuts?" said Nora.

"You're a pretty good spy, Beatrice."

"No," said Beatrice. I'm a *super* spy."